Oceania

Jennifer Prior, Ph.D.

Consultants

Kerry Shannon, Ph.D.
Assistant Professor of History
California State University, Dominguez Hills

Gloria Brown
New South Wales, Australia

Jon Anger
English, History, and ELD Teacher
Novato Unified School District

Publishing Credits

Rachelle Cracchiolo, M.S.Ed., *Publisher*
Emily R. Smith, M.A.Ed., *SVP of Content Development*
Véronique Bos, *Vice President of Creative*
Dani Neiley, *Editor*
Fabiola Sepulveda, *Series Graphic Designer*

Image Credits: p.12 Wikimedia John Webber; p.13 © Look and Learn/Bridgeman Images; p.15 Alamy/James Davis Photography; p.16 (top) Bridgeman Images; p.16 (bottom) Alamy/Operation 2021; p.18 (top) Alamy/Allstar Picture Library Ltd; p.19 (top) Parliament of Australia Royal Collection (RCIN 407587); p.20 Alamy/ZUMA Press, Inc; p.21 (bottom) Alamy/Jeremy Sutton-Hibbert; p.27 (top) Shutterstock/Jixiang Liu; all other images from iStock and/or Shutterstock

Library of Congress Cataloging-in-Publication Data

Names: Prior, Jennifer Overend, 1963- author.
Title: Oceania / Jennifer Prior, PhD.
Description: Huntington Beach, CA : Teacher Created Materials, Inc, [2023]
| Includes index. | Audience: Ages 8-18 | Summary: "Oceania is vast and includes thousands of islands. It is home to the large island continent of Australia, as well as the third smallest island in the world. It is also home to many tribal groups. Many people travel to Oceania for great scuba diving, but there is so much more to know about this vast part of the world"-- Provided by publisher.
Identifiers: LCCN 2022038399 (print) | LCCN 2022038400 (ebook) | ISBN 9781087695198 (paperback) | ISBN 9781087695358 (ebook)
Subjects: LCSH: Oceania--Juvenile literature.
Classification: LCC DU347 .P75 2023 (print) | LCC DU517 (ebook) | DDC 995--dc23/eng/20220823
LC record available at https://lccn.loc.gov/2022038399
LC ebook record available at https://lccn.loc.gov/2022038400

Shown on the cover is the island of
Bora-Bora.

This book may not be reproduced or distributed in any
way without prior written consent from the publisher.

5482 Argosy Avenue
Huntington Beach, CA 92649
www.tcmpub.com
ISBN 978-1-0876-9519-8
© 2023 Teacher Created Materials, Inc.

Table of Contents

Way Out in the South Pacific 4
Where in the World? 6
Indigenous Peoples of Oceania 10
Modern Life 14
Hail the King…or Queen! 18
Getting Involved 20
Economies in Oceania 22
Vast and Unique 26
Map It! 28
Glossary 30
Index 31
Learn More! 32

Sydney, Australia

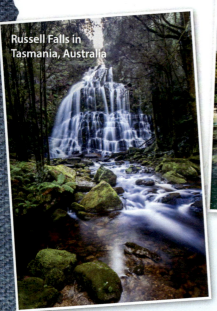

Russell Falls in Tasmania, Australia

Upolu, Samoa

Pacific Ocean

NORTHERN MARIANA ISLANDS (United States)

Philippine Sea

GUAM (United States)

MARSHALL ISLANDS

PALAU

FEDERATED STATES OF MICRONESIA

KIR

Micronesia

NAURU

* As a whole, this island is called New Guinea.

INDONESIA

PAPUA NEW GUINEA

SOLOMON ISLANDS

Melanesia

VANUATU

Coral Sea

NEW CALEDONIA (France)

AUSTRALIA

Indian Ocean

Australasia

TASMANIA

Tasman Sea

NEW ZEALAND

Way Out in the South Pacific

Way out in the South Pacific Ocean is a string of thousands of islands. The surrounding blue waters are filled with a variety of marine life. Each island is unique. The people have varied cultures and languages.

This area is called *Oceania*. There are four island regions in Oceania. Two are Australasia and Micronesia. The other two are Melanesia and Polynesia.

Long, long ago, the islands in this area were difficult places for humans to survive. There were few resources and little to eat. So, when people settled there, they brought plants and animals with them. People on these islands dealt with harsh weather as well. Cyclones, also known as hurricanes, have hit many of these islands hard. But the people of Oceania are strong and **resilient** against these challenges.

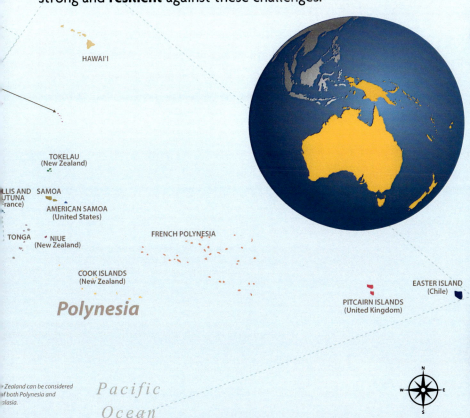

Rainbow Valley Conservation Reserve, Australia

Where in the World?

The islands of Oceania sit in the central and southern Pacific Ocean. Australia is the largest island. It is one of the world's seven continents. The second-largest island is New Guinea. Part of Indonesia makes up the western half of New Guinea. Papua New Guinea makes up the eastern half. New Zealand is the third-largest island in Oceania. The rest of the islands are much smaller in comparison. There are thousands of them. A large number of them are uninhabited. This means people do not live there.

The wildlife and plants in Oceania are diverse. Many of the islands have plants and animals that exist nowhere else on Earth. They are completely unique to the area. Kangaroos are one example. They are only native to Australia and Papua New Guinea.

Tongariro Alpine Crossing, New Zealand

The islands of Oceania have different physical features. Australia, New Zealand, and New Guinea are called *continental islands*. They were once connected to other land masses. They broke away as a result of movements in the earth.

Australasia

Australasia consists of Australia and the state of Tasmania. There is a wide range of terrain across the continent. A great portion of Australia is desert. Some people call this the *Outback*. Other parts of Australia get a lot of rain. This is especially true in parts of Tasmania. Rain forests can be found there.

Hidden under the Surface

Zealandia is a large land mass that is almost completely underwater. Zealandia is half the size of Australia. New Zealand is the largest portion that sits above the water. Small islands or rocks, such as Ball's Pyramid, sit above the water, too.

Ball's Pyramid

Melanesia

Melanesia is a group of islands created from volcanic activity. Volcanic eruptions pushed the earth above the ocean's surface. This formed small land masses. These islands are known as high islands. Out of this group, only New Guinea did not form this way. It was created by plates of the earth's crust colliding. This region also includes the Solomon Islands and Fiji.

Navala Village, Fiji

Micronesia

Micronesia consists of some islands formed by volcanoes. Others are formed by coral. Coral is made up of small ocean animals. They look like plants. But they are very hard, almost like stone. Coral islands are also called *low islands*. They are formed from the skeletons of coral. This region includes the Marshall Islands and Guam.

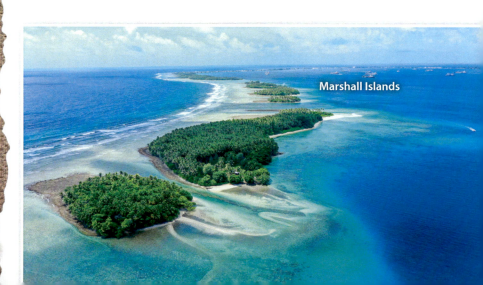
Marshall Islands

Haleakalā National Park, Hawai'i

Polynesia

Polynesia also has some volcanic islands. But more of them are coral islands. It is common to find groups of small islands. These are called *atolls*. They surround **lagoons**. This region includes New Zealand, Tahiti, Samoa, and the Hawaiian Islands.

Oceania's Smallest Island

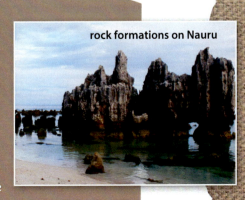
rock formations on Nauru

Oceania consists of 14 countries and more than 10,000 islands. A few of the islands are large, but most are quite small. The smallest island nation is Nauru. It is only 8 square miles (21 square kilometers). As of 2021, the population was roughly 10,873 people.

Indigenous Peoples of Oceania

The number of Indigenous peoples in Oceania is far less than other regions of the world. But there are still many Indigenous cultures there. Each one has its own history and **customs**.

Aborigines

There are 500 groups of Aboriginal peoples in Australia alone. Each group has its own land and language. They have strong spiritual connections to the land. The Aboriginal peoples also create a lot of art. Some of it explores their connection to the land. Body art is common. This involves painting their skin with bright colors. They have many ceremonies throughout the year that involve music and dancing. Close to half the people have held onto their traditional lifestyles and customs. Today, some of them live near the coast. Others live in the desert (called the *bush*). More than half the Aboriginal peoples live in cities and towns.

three generations of an Aboriginal family

Boys walk to school in Fiji.

Highlands tribe members in Papua New Guinea

Melanesians

Melanesia consists of many islands and cultures. As a whole, the people are referred to as Papuans. Papuans have lived in this region for thousands of years. Oral tradition, or storytelling, is important to people there. Hundreds of different languages are still spoken there today. One of the most common languages is Fijian. It is an official language of Fiji, and it is used throughout the country. Newspapers and government publications use this language.

Dance to the Beat

The *kundu* is a drum used by tribal groups in Melanesia. The kundu is shaped like an hourglass and is used in ceremonies and celebrations. People sing and dance to the beat of this drum.

a Samoan man at a Polynesian cultural center

Polynesians

People first made their way to the Polynesian islands from East and Southeast Asia. The islands of Polynesia are spread across thousands of miles. So, people traveled in canoes with big sails to get there. They brought many plants and animals with them. This helped them survive. This was especially true on islands that had few resources. The people spread across these islands shared a common cultural **heritage**.

Polynesians were boat builders. They were skilled farmers. And they made functional and artistic items from wood. Early Polynesians were **pagan**. But **missionaries** came to the islands in the late 1700s. Today, most of the people are Christians.

illustration of Hawaiian navigators sailing across a bay

Large stones were used as money in the Yap Islands in Micronesia.

Micronesians

The people in this region are broadly known as Micronesians. There are many cultures within this group. Some people throughout the region speak Indigenous languages. There are many different **dialects**. In Palau, the Federated States of Micronesia, and Guam, English is widely used. Most people in this region are Christians. Most of them live, work, and go to school in towns. Traditional ways of life are usually only followed on the outer islands of the region.

The Presence of the Past

There is a long history of **colonization** in Oceania. Australia is just one example. In the late 1700s, the British government claimed Australia as its own. They took over Aboriginal land. The British government made laws. In time, Australia broke away from Great Britain. It claimed independence. But its style of government still has some British influence.

Modern Life

Each country in Oceania has its own unique culture.

Australia

Australians are described as "down-to-earth and friendly." They love the outdoors, and surfing is a popular sport. Cricket is another popular sport played with a bat and a ball. People in Australia also love spending time with friends and family, and they like to have barbecues. You may hear a barbecue called "the barbie."

game of cricket

The arts and storytelling are popular in Australia. There are several well-known arts and Aboriginal arts festivals throughout the year. Some people like to play the *didjeridu*. This is an instrument that looks like a long trumpet.

New Zealand

The culture of New Zealand is influenced by the European lifestyle. But customs of native peoples are also common to see. In recent decades, there has been an emphasis on creativity. The people value the arts. The country even provides **grants** to its people. The grants encourage people to engage in music and dance as well as art and writing. People from the Māori culture love to entertain guests. And they are open about sharing their customs. They, too, value artistic skills. In particular, they do wood carvings and weaving.

Māori family

Samoa

Life in Samoa centers around traditional customs. They value music, dance, and storytelling. Tattoos have great meaning to the people. They even have tattooing ceremonies. These permanent markings on the skin reflect the people's history. A traditional tattoo is called a *pe'a*. Some young men get this tattoo. It covers their body from mid-torso to their knees. It is thought to be disrespectful for an outsider to get a Samoan tattoo.

pe'a

Matariki

Matariki is a holiday that is celebrated every year in New Zealand. It marks the start of the Māori New Year. This is when the Matariki star cluster appears in the sky. The cluster is also known as Pleiades. In 2022, Matariki became an official public holiday in New Zealand. It is a day of remembrance. People also celebrate the year to come.

surfers in Hawai'i, 1910

Hawai'i

Hawaiians came to the islands on sailing canoes. They were farmers and fishers. Hawai'i was once its own country. The people were ruled by kings. The first ruler, King Kamehameha, united the islands.

Aloha, which means "hello" and "goodbye," is considered a way of life in Hawai'i. The aloha spirit is about relationships. It's about showing kindness.

Guam

Guam is a **territory** of the United States. It has a mix of cultures. People in Guam celebrate U.S. holidays. Guam also has influences from Spain and the native CHamoru people. The CHamoru are a respected group of people. It is common to see their traditional dances and hear their music in Guam.

CHamoru dancers perform in Guam.

Children perform a traditional dance in Fiji.

Fiji

Fiji is extremely **diverse**. It is a place where people from different races and religions live peacefully together. Native Fijians love music, dance, and food. They use dance to tell stories of their people. Traditional food is cooked in an underground oven called a *lovo*. Imagine the taste of sweet potatoes, pork, or fish. Add spices and a hint of smoke. Now you have food from Fiji!

What's a Territory?

A territory is land that is governed by another country. American Samoa is a territory of the United States. Guam is another U.S. territory. It was once owned by Spain. But the United States took political control after the Spanish-American War in 1898.

Hail the King...or Queen!

A monarchy is a form of government. A king or queen is at the head of the government. They are part of a royal family.

In Oceania, there are six constitutional monarchies. In most of these, the king or queen does not make political decisions. They are not involved in the lawmaking process. That job is for Parliament or the local leaders.

The monarch of the United Kingdom is the head of state for five of these monarchies. This includes Australia, New Zealand, and Papua New Guinea. This is true for the Solomon Islands and Tuvalu as well.

The Kingdom of Tonga has its own monarchy. The king is head of state. He is also the leader of the military.

Queen Elizabeth II, longest-reigning British monarch

New Zealand Parliament

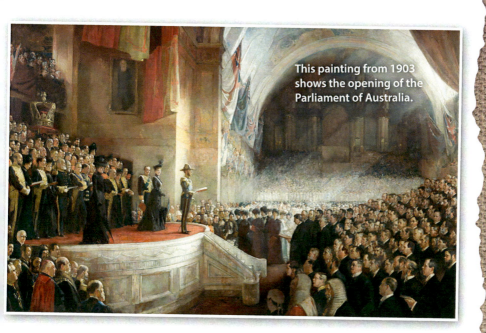

This painting from 1903 shows the opening of the Parliament of Australia.

Parliamentary Systems

Some countries in Oceania have parliamentary government systems. These are democratic systems that represent the people. There is an elected prime minister. This person is the leader over the whole country. Other leaders are elected to Parliament. This is a group that makes laws and decisions. And there are leaders elected to run states or smaller regions. All these people work for the good of the country. New Zealand and Australia have these types of systems.

Representative Democracy

Not all countries in Oceania have parliamentary systems. One example is the Federated States of Micronesia. It has a representative democracy. It separates powers into three branches. They are the legislative, executive, and judicial. A president and vice president lead the country. They are elected by the National Congress.

Getting Involved

Getting people involved in their communities is strongly stressed throughout Oceania. Many chiefs in Micronesia have taken the leads in their small villages. They promote health and living a good life. They also want their people to be involved. Whether in villages or in cities, people throughout Oceania are finding causes to participate in.

In Melanesia, young people take interest in their communities. They want to see positive change. Technology and social media have helped. Young people focus on the issues of their people. They learn about these through social media and text messages.

A political candidate talks about politics with students at a school in Hawai'i.

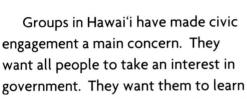
Cleaning up litter is one way young people can get involved in their communities.

Sea turtles confuse plastic bags with jellyfish.

Groups in Hawai'i have made civic engagement a main concern. They want all people to take an interest in government. They want them to learn how it works. And they want them to have a voice. Project Citizen and Kids Voting Hawai'i are two successful programs. They encourage children to learn about making policies. They also give children ways to help with elections.

Young people in Fiji are also becoming **activists**. They work together in groups. They comment on local plans. They create ways for young people to get involved. These children hope to inspire other young people to work toward a better future.

Climate Change

Climate change is causing sea levels to rise. For Oceania, this is a big problem. Someday, they could be completely underwater. Some people in Oceania **advocate** for laws to be passed to reduce the effects of climate change. They also want to bring international attention to the issue.

A man uses sandbags as protection against rising sea levels in Kiribati.

Economies in Oceania

Australia and New Zealand have the largest and strongest economies in Oceania. The other island nations are much smaller. Their economies are smaller, and there may be fewer job opportunities. Typically, people in Oceania work to produce **goods**. They also provide services.

Australia

This country is extremely dry with very little rain. And it has poor soil quality. So, farming is difficult. Even still, wheat is a successful crop. It is used to make bread and noodles. Australia has a successful sheep **industry** as well. The country provides the world with more wool than any other country does. Companies in Australia

sheep shearing

earn money from the mining of minerals and metals. Other businesses provide services, such as banking and education. And people in Australia make goods in factories. Some of them are exported around the world. This includes cars and textiles.

gold mining, Australia

movie set, New Zealand

New Zealand

New Zealand has a few popular industries. First, farming is a big business in New Zealand. Farmers export wool from sheep. They also produce milk, butter, and cheese. Fishing is another large industry. Paper and other wood products are also made there. Finally, businesses in the country also earn quite a bit of money from tourism. People from all over the world love to visit the national parks. Some people visit the Lord of the Rings and The Hobbit movie sets. The popular movies were filmed there.

fisherman in New Zealand

Earthquake!

New Zealand is near many **fault lines**. Because of this, it experiences an extremely high number of earthquakes. In fact, there are about 15,000 earthquakes every year! Some of them are small and not noticeable. But close to 150 of them each year can be felt. These can cause significant damage. This has a huge impact on the economy. Building and road repairs can be costly.

The other countries in Oceania are very small. Some of them have limited job opportunities. Certain islands have lots of farmland, and the people there grow crops. Other islands do not have much farmland, so people work fishing jobs instead.

Natural disasters can affect their economies. Oceania experiences tropical cyclones and earthquakes. These fierce storms damage homes and roads. They can cause flooding. It is often very expensive to rebuild from these disasters. But the countries and their economies are resilient.

Melanesia

Most countries in this region depend on fishing and forestry. They also rely on tourism. People often visit for beach vacations. They come to enjoy snorkeling and scuba diving. In Fiji, you can dive and swim with sharks! Many locals have jobs that provide services for visitors.

Micronesia

In the countries in this region, most people farm and fish for their own families. These islands have few natural resources. Food, fuel, and other goods have to be imported. Some people work as fishers. Fish is a main export in the region. **Infrastructure** is continuing to develop. Tourism is on the rise, especially in Palau. This island country has famous dive sites that draw visitors from around the world.

coral reef in Fiji

Bora-Bora

Polynesia

Much of this region relies on tourism. And a lot of people visit each year. Tahiti, Bora-Bora, and the Hawaiian Islands are popular vacation spots. Most of these islands have rich soil and mild climates. This makes them perfect for farming. Hawai'i, in particular, has a lot of farms. Farmers in the state grow sugarcane, pineapple, and papaya. They also grow coffee and macadamia nuts.

Subsistence Farming

Some people grow food or raise animals just for themselves. This is called *subsistence farming*. These people usually have only a few acres of land. They do not grow or raise food on a large scale or sell it to earn money. Many people across Oceania are subsistence farmers.

Vast and Unique

Oceania is a **vast** area. The ocean water is clear and blue. Its islands are as unique as the people who live there.

The culture is a unique mix, too. There are numerous Indigenous groups. And there are also descendants of English, French, Spanish, and German people who colonized the region long ago. Some tribal people still enjoy their traditional ways of life. Festivals and holidays bring some of these traditions to modern life. People from all backgrounds are united in the four regions of Oceania.

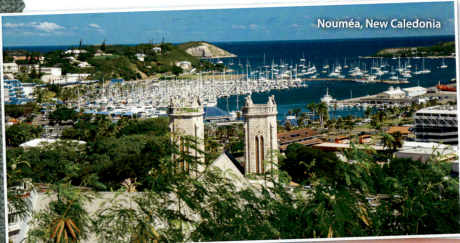

Nouméa, New Caledonia

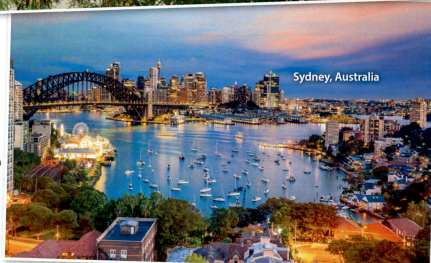

Sydney, Australia

The arts are highly valued across these countries. Music, dance, art, and even tattoos express creativity and culture. People often gather for festivals hosted by different countries. This serves to bring people together who would otherwise be isolated from one another.

Māori artist working on a wood carving

Each island nation has its own economy. In some countries, people make and sell wool and dairy products. Some crops grown by farmers are exported around the world. And across Oceania, tourism is important. National parks and beautiful beaches bring in visitors.

Oceania continues to make significant contributions to the world. It is a place like no other.

French Polynesia

Land of the Few

Most of Oceania is made up of water. Only 43 million people live there. That sounds like a lot, but it's really not. This part of the world is sparsely populated. In fact, there are likely more sheep in the area than people!

Map It!

Now that you've learned about the regions of Oceania, it's time to make a map! Work together with a group to make a map of one region in Oceania.

1. Choose one region of Oceania: Australasia, Micronesia, Melanesia, or Polynesia.

2. Make a map of it on poster board. Draw the outline of your region. Name and label the countries.

3. Do research online. Identify the ocean surrounding it, and name several of the islands. (Some regions have hundreds of islands—try to name at least ten.)

4. Find and label the locations of at least five major cities or towns.

5. Choose one other fact to include about the region on your map. You may write about the Indigenous peoples who can be found there, which types of crops are grown, or which tourist destinations are popular.

sheep in New Zealand

Glossary

activists—people who take strong action to make changes in politics or society

advocate—to support and fight for a cause

colonization—the process of a distant country taking over and controlling an area

customs—behaviors that are usual and traditional among people in a particular group or area

dialects—forms of language that are spoken by certain groups

diverse—made up of people or things that are different from one another

fault lines—long cracks in the earth's surface where earthquakes tend to occur

goods—products people buy

grants—money given to people by a government or company to be used for certain purposes

heritage—traditions that are a part of the history of a group

industry—a group of businesses that provide a particular product or service

infrastructure—the system of public works in an area, such as roads and bridges

lagoons—shallow ponds of water that are connected to or near larger bodies of water

missionaries—people who travel to a foreign country to do religious work

pagan—people who do not follow the religions of Islam, Christianity, or Judaism

resilient—able to recover from difficulties

territory—an area of land ruled or governed by another country

vast—great in size

paddleboarding in French Polynesia

Index

Aborigines, 10

American Samoa, 5, 17

Australasia, 4–6

Australia, 4–7, 10, 13–14, 18–19, 22, 24, 26

Bora-Bora, 25

CHamoru, 16

Cook Islands, 5

Elizabeth II, 18

Federated States of Micronesia, 4, 13, 19

Fiji, 4, 8, 11, 17, 21, 24

French Polynesia, 5, 27

Guam, 4, 8, 16–17

Hawaiʻi, 5–6, 9, 12, 16, 20, 21, 25

Indonesia, 4–5

Kiribati, 4–5, 21

Māori, 14, 27

Marshall Islands, 4, 8

Melanesia, 4, 5, 8, 11, 20, 24

Micronesia, 4–5, 8, 13, 20, 24

Nauru, 4, 9

New Caledonia, 4, 26

New Guinea, 4, 6–8

New Zealand, 4–7, 9, 14–15, 18–19, 22–23

Niue, 5

Northern Mariana Islands, 4

Palau, 4, 13, 24

Papua New Guinea, 4, 6, 11, 18

Papuans, 11

Polynesia, 5, 9, 12, 25

Samoa, 4–5, 9, 12, 15

Solomon Islands, 4, 8, 18

Tahiti, 9, 25

Tasmania, 4, 7

Tonga, 5, 18

Tuvalu, 4, 18

Vanuatu, 4

Learn More!

Richard (Dick) Smith is a successful Australian businessman and entrepreneur. He founded a company called Dick Smith Electronics. He is also an aviator and has set many world records. Research to answer the questions, and create a booklet about him.

- What world records has he set in aviation?
- What is an entrepreneur?
- He is described as a philanthropist. What is that?
- What good things does he do with his money?
- Find one other interesting fact about him.

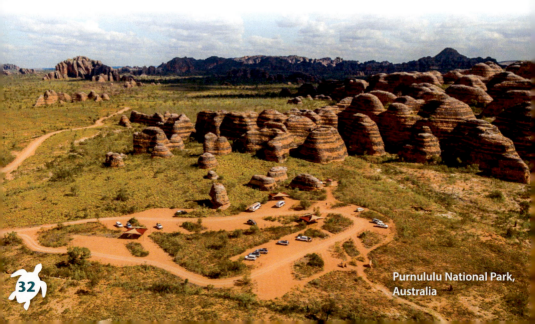

Purnululu National Park, Australia